S0-CYE-892

TORNADOES

CHARLES ROTTER

CREATIVE EDUCATION

Designed by Rita Marshall
with the help of Melinda Belter

Published by Creative Education,
123 South Broad Street, Mankato,
Minnesota 56001.

Creative Education is an imprint of
The Creative Company

Photography by Comstock, Gerry Ellis,
Peter Arnold, Inc., Photo Researchers,
Stock Market, and Tom Stack, Inc.,

Library of Congress
Cataloging-in-Publication Data

Rotter, Charles.
Tornadoes / Charles Rotter.

    p.   cm.
ISBN 0-88682-712-4
1. Tornadoes–Juvenile literature.
[1. Tornadoes.]   I. Title.   93-46803

QC955.2.R68   1997   CIP
551.55'3–dc20   AC

5 4 3 2 1

Printed in Hong Kong

6

Earth's winds serve many important and welcome functions. In steamy tropical lands, mild breezes help ventilate homes and relieve otherwise stifling conditions. In colder climates, warm springtime winds help melt snow and ice and hurry the change of seasons. Wind energy is used to sail boats and to operate mills; wind-powered generators are used to produce electricity.

Although we have learned to appreciate the wind and to use it to our advantage, it remains a largely uncontrollable force of nature. Wind can suddenly turn from kindly benefactor to angry oppressor in the form of atmospheric storms. Of all of the storms that batter our planet, perhaps none strike more suddenly or with more deadly force than the *Tornado.*

Wind harnessed by man.

Tornadoes are spinning columns of air that descend from thunderstorm clouds like long fingers reaching toward the earth. They get their name from the Latin word *tornare*, which means "to turn." The spinning, funnel-like shape of a tornado has been described as looking like a tree trunk, a mushroom stem, or even an elephant's trunk. A tornado may appear dark from swirling soil and debris, or it may take on a distinct color depending on the type of soil spinning within it. Its frightening roar has been likened to the sound of a million angry bees, a thousand jumbo jets, and screaming locomotive engines.

Many stories have been told about bizarre happenings during tornadoes, and all attest to the power and unpredictability of these swirling winds. Chickens have been stripped of their feathers; rivers have been temporarily sucked dry; straw has been driven deep into tree trunks. Pieces of wood, from splinters to entire boards, have been punched through steel poles and buildings. Like giant vacuum cleaners, tornadoes have sucked up railroad cars and tossed them about like toys. People and animals have been picked up and deposited some distance away, some fortunate ones still alive.

At the mercy of wind.

Meteorologists, or scientists who study weather, do not fully understand tornadoes. But meteorologists do know that the same conditions that spawn severe thunderstorms also give rise to tornadoes: unstable air, high humidity, and the clashing together of low-level winds. When air coming from two different directions meets and pushes upward, it is referred to as a *Convergence of Air.* Because warm air is lighter than cold air, it rises while cold air falls. The air masses rotate around each other and fight for position along a boundary line called a *Front.* Rapidly rising moist air forms *Cumulonimbus Clouds,* better known as thunderheads. Clouds often produce violent rainstorms accompanied by lightning and thunder.

A thunderhead.

When air rises during a thunderstorm, air pressure drops, creating a low-pressure area. Surrounding air then rushes in to equalize these unstable conditions and pushes more air upward. Factors such as the earth's rotation and the *Jet Stream*—high-speed winds far above the earth—force this air into a swirling vortex, or whirl, called an *Anticyclone.* In the Northern Hemisphere, anticyclones spin counterclockwise; in the Southern Hemisphere they spin clockwise.

As air in an anticyclone moves inward toward the area of low pressure, the energy of rotation, called *Angular Momentum,* becomes concentrated into a smaller and smaller area. The air moves faster and faster, creating high winds and, frequently, tornadoes. Unfortunately, wind-measuring devices are destroyed along with everything else in a tornado's path, so exact measurements are difficult to obtain. But based on theory and engineering damage estimates, scientists believe that rotational wind speeds can reach 300 miles (483 km) per hour or greater. Some wind speeds may be even greater, because the movement of the whole tornado increases the wind speed within the tornado.

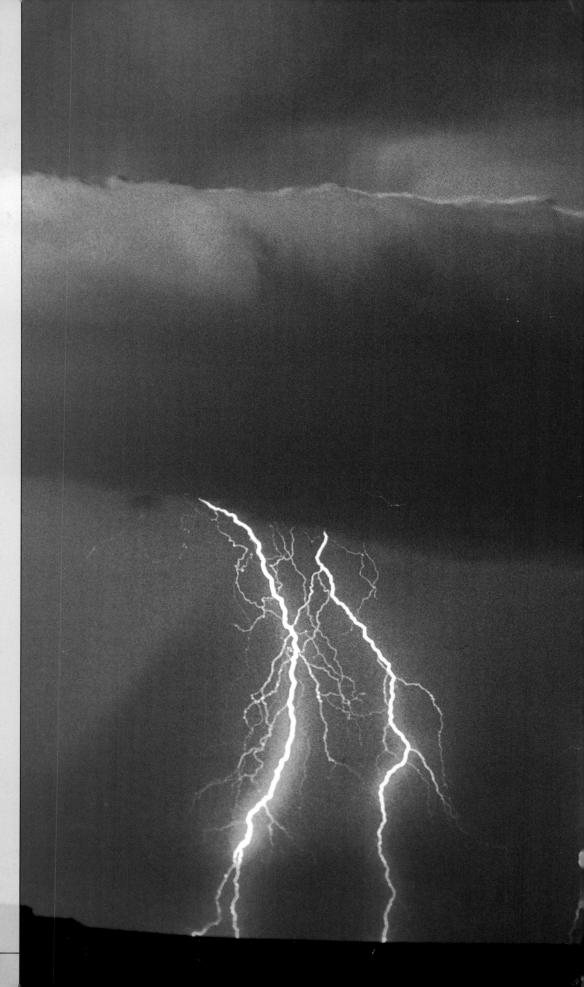

Electrical storm in Texas panhandle.

Tornadoes occur all over the world, but the greatest number—sometimes 1,000 in a single year—strike in North America. Australia takes second place with several hundred tornadoes annually, but because most of the continent is sparsely populated, many may go unreported. Tornadoes also occur in New Zealand, Italy, and England, and have been reported as far north as Stockholm, Sweden. Tropical regions also suffer from tornadoes, but these are usually associated with hurricanes and are less severe than tornadoes in temperate climates. Historical data indicates that tornado reportings are increasing, but this may have more to do with expanding populations and improved reporting than with actual increases in tornado numbers.

Tornadoes don't confine themselves to land. Sometimes they form over lakes or oceans. These tornadoes are referred to as *Waterspouts* because the bottom part of the funnel consists mainly of spray. Waterspouts are most common in tropical oceans and are generally smaller in size and have less violent winds than land tornadoes.

Waterspout in the tropics.

16

In the United States, tornadoes strike every state, including Alaska and Hawaii, but by far the most frequented areas are the central and southeastern portions of the country. In fact, the entire central region from Texas to Minnesota is referred to as *Tornado Alley*. During spring and summer months, warm, moist air from the Gulf of Mexico moves northward up the Mississippi Valley and collides with cold, dry air flowing south from Canada. This sets up the perfect environment for thunderstorms and tornadoes.

Tornado on the prairie.

Texas reports the largest number of tornadoes, but that is due in part to its large size. Another way to measure tornado occurrence is by the average number of tornadoes per unit area, such as square mile or square kilometer. If tornado frequency is measured in this way, Kansas and Oklahoma record the most tornadoes. Potential casualties depend both on tornado frequency and population density. Southwest Oklahoma has the highest tornado incidence per unit area, but a low population. Even though Chicago experiences half the number of tornadoes per unit area as compared with southwestern Oklahoma, it has a higher casualty potential because it is much more heavily populated.

Tornadoes can strike during any season, but spring and summer months have five times as many tornadoes as fall and winter. More than half of all tornadoes occurring in the United States strike during the months of April, May, and June. Tornadoes have struck at all hours of day and night, but most form during the afternoon or early evening, when the ground is warmest. They usually, but not always, travel from southwest to northeast.

Evening tornado.

Tornadoes are sometimes called *Twisters* because they twist and turn on their grim, unpredictable path. They generally move forward at a speed of 30 miles (48 km) per hour, but they often zigzag, make abrupt turns, or even stay in one place for several minutes. A swirling funnel may destroy several homes on a city block, retreat into the sky, and then touch down again a few blocks away. Tornadoes are also capable of striking the same place twice. Sometimes several tornadoes emerge from the same storm cloud and travel in rotating clusters, frequently changing the leader as the dangerous group moves along.

Although tornadoes spend a relatively short time on the ground, usually 10 minutes or less, and travel an average of just 15 miles (24 km) before dissipating, they can cause tremendous destruction. A storm lasting just minutes can leave people homeless, destroy businesses and jobs, and dole out death and serious injuries.

Page 20: Multiple waterspouts.
Page 21: Dust climbs the neck of a tornado.

22

Besides high winds, tornadoes cause damage in other ways not nearly as obvious. Air pressure inside a tornado is extremely low. As it passes over a building, the difference between the inside and outside air pressures can be great enough to shatter windows or even blow roofs from buildings. The structures are then so weakened that the powerful winds accompanying the storm easily destroy what remains. Strong updrafts of air can also pull trees from the ground and lift buildings from their foundations.

Terrible destruction by a tornado.

The record books bear witness to the fury of these intense storms. The largest outbreak of tornadoes ever recorded occurred on April 3 and 4, 1974, when a group of 148 tornadoes terrorized 13 states in the eastern, southern, and midwestern United States, as well as a small part of Canada. The "Super Outbreak," as it is called, took 315 lives and caused more than $600 million in damage. In terms of lost lives, the most deadly tornadoes occurred on March 18, 1925, when 689 people were killed in Missouri, Illinois, and Indiana. Another destructive group of tornadoes formed in April 1965. The cluster of about 47 tornadoes smashed its way through Indiana, Illinois, Iowa, Wisconsin, Ohio, and Michigan. Along the way it killed 271 people, injured thousands, and caused roughly $300 million in property damage.

The outer edge of a tornado.

While we cannot control the violent action of tornadoes, we have made much progress in predicting their development. Advanced computer and radar systems now help warn people of conditions favoring tornadoes. Meteorologists use *Doppler Radar*, a forecasting system that accurately measures wind speed during a thunderstorm and detects rotating winds. They also use satellites to monitor clouds and help predict the formation of tornadoes. The major benefit of these systems is that of advanced warning: they allow people adequate time to take shelter.

Stratocumulus clouds at sea.

If conditions are right for tornadoes, the United States National Weather Service issues a *Tornado Watch* for a specific area and time. People living within watch areas are advised to listen to their radios for further weather developments. Should a tornado be spotted by human eye or radar, a *Tornado Warning* is issued, and civil defense sirens warn residents to seek shelter immediately.

When emergency sirens announce a tornado warning, it is very important to take cover quickly. Storm cellars and basements offer the best protection. In a basement, people should curl up in a fetal position under a concrete stairway, a heavy work bench, or a table in the middle of the room to help protect themselves from injury if the house collapses. In a house with no basement, the safest place is a bathtub or small closet in the middle of the house. A small mattress, such as one from a crib, can be pulled over the bathtub as additional protection from debris.

~

Staying outside to watch a tornado might be exciting, but it isn't smart. People who are in cars or outdoors when a tornado strikes should seek shelter in a nearby building. If no building is near, they should lie down flat in a ditch. Culverts should be avoided, however, as they may quickly fill with water during the heavy rains that often accompany tornadoes. Residents in mobile homes should go to a shelter in the mobile home park and wait for the storm to pass.

Tornado cell signals a warning.

We have learned to alter many parts of the natural world to fit our needs, but earth's weather systems, including its destructive storms, still escape our control. While we mourn the loss of life and property caused by *Tornadoes*, we must also respect the awesome display of nature's power. With all of our technological advances, in the end we must concede that nature's spectacular forces answer not to us, but we to them.

Tornado approaching.